To Gisèle, Caillou's godmother
C.L.

Caillou

Sometimes Moms Get Angry

Text: Christine L'Heureux • Consultant: Francine Nadeau, M. Psych., child psychologist
Illustrations: Pierre Brignaud • Coloration: Marcel Depratto

chouette

Caillou is shopping for new shoes with his mommy today. In the store, he sees another mother with her baby and her little girl.
The little girl knocks a shoe off the display table.

"Come here! Pick that shoe up and put it back where it belongs," the mother orders the little girl in a loud voice. The girl goes toward the shoe, she looks at her mother and then she turns away to play. Caillou watches them. He can hardly move.

The mother takes her daughter firmly by the arm and makes her bend down.
"Do what I tell you!" the mother says harshly.
The little girl picks up the shoe, but drops it again.
"Oh!" says Caillou. He is startled.

The mother grabs her daughter's arm
and hurries out of the store.
The little girl cries as she runs after her.
"Wow, the mommy is really angry! That
scares me," Caillou says, looking at his
own mother.

When they get back in the car, Mommy says to Caillou, "You were very upset when you saw the angry mommy in the store. You know, sometimes mothers forget that their children are only little."
Caillou listens without saying anything.

Mommy bends over Caillou and pats
his cheek.
"Sometimes I get angry, too, and it frightens
you. I don't seem to be the mommy you
know. It might even make you think of
a witch."
Caillou is a bit shocked.

"You can tell me if I speak too loudly. I don't want to frighten you when I get angry. I still love you, even when I'm not happy with what you do," Mommy adds. Caillou continues to listen without saying anything.

"Sometimes I'm tired and I get really annoyed," Mommy says. "You don't deserve that."
Caillou looks at Mommy, and then he looks down.
He whispers, "Sometimes, I pretend to block my ears. I stop listening so I won't be too scared."

When they get home, Caillou goes to his room to play. He wants to finish building his racetrack.

Daddy calls him from the kitchen, but Caillou is very busy and doesn't hear Daddy.

Daddy goes upstairs and stands at Caillou's bedroom door.

"Come and eat, Caillou. We're all at the table," Daddy says gently.

Caillou hasn't finished his construction project, but he wants to please his daddy.

Caillou decides to stop everything to go and eat.

"I love you, Daddy," Caillou says.

"I love you, too, Caillou. You're my big boy."

© 2013 CHOUETTE PUBLISHING (1987) INC.
CAILLOU is a registered trademark of Chouette Publishing (1987) Inc.
Text: Christine L'Heureux
Consultant: Francine Nadeau, M. Psych., child psychologist
Illustrations: Pierre Brignaud
Coloration: Marcel Depratto

The PBS KIDS logo is a registered mark of PBS and is used with permission.

We acknowledge the financial support of the Government of Canada through the Canada Book Fund for our publishing activities.

We acknowledge the support of the Ministry of Culture and Communications of Quebec and SODEC for the publication and promotion of this book.

Canadian Heritage Patrimoine canadien

SODEC
Québec

Bibliothèque et Archives nationales du Québec and Library and Archives Canada cataloguing in publication

L'heureux, Christine, 1946-
[Caillou: parfois, les mamans se fâchent. English]
Caillou: sometimes moms get angry
(Hand in hand)Translation of: Caillou: parfois, les mamans se fâchent.
For children aged 2 and up.
ISBN 978-2-89718-116-1

1. Anger - Juvenile literature. 2. Fear - Juvenile literature. I. Brignaud, Pierre. II. Title. III. Title: Caillou: parfois, les mamans se fâchent. English. IV. Series: Hand in hand (Montréal, Québec).

BF575.A5L4313 2014   j152.4'7   C2013-941965-9

Printed in Shenzhen, China
10 9 8 7 6 5 4 3 2 1   CHO1895 OCT2013

Hand in Hand
Milestones in child development

See the entire collection
www.chouette.co